PLEASE WASH YOUR HANDS
BEFORE READING ME.

SUHO AND THE WHITE HORSE

A LEGEND OF MONGOLIA

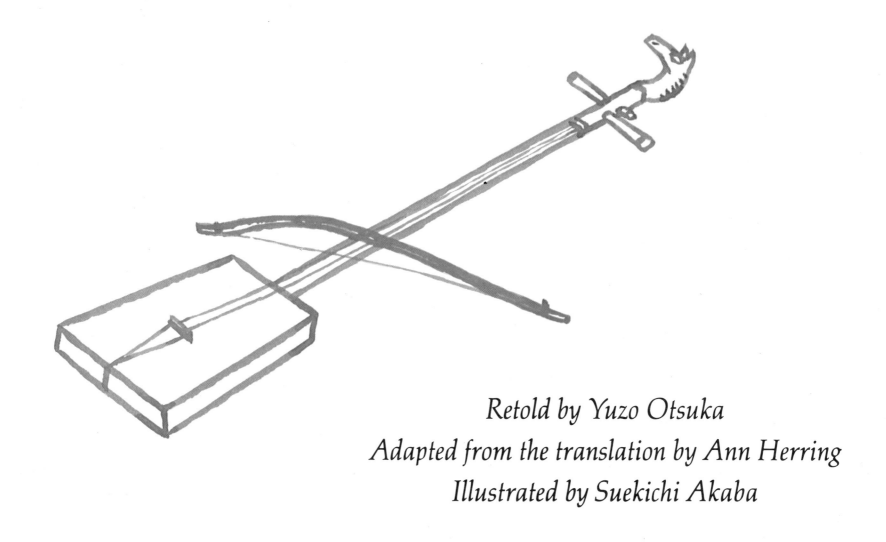

Retold by Yuzo Otsuka

Adapted from the translation by Ann Herring

Illustrated by Suekichi Akaba

THE VIKING PRESS   NEW YORK

In the heart of Asia lies an ancient land called
Mongolia. Its broad steppes and grasslands have long
been the home of brave horsemen and shepherds. Among
the people of Mongolia, many play a beautiful instrument
called a horse-head fiddle, which takes its name from the
small figure of a horse's head carved at the top.

 If the carved horse's head could speak
to you, this is the tale it would tell.

Long ago a poor shepherd boy named Suho lived with his grandmother in a round *yurt*, or roomy felt tent, in the middle of the Mongolian steppes. Each day Suho rose early, to help his grandmother and to prepare breakfast. Then he would go out onto the grassy plains to watch over their small flock of sheep.

Suho loved to sing. His rich voice would often ring out over the steppes, breaking the stillness of early evening.

One night Suho did not return to his grandmother's *yurt* at the usual time.
His grandmother and the other shepherds were frantic with worry.

Then all at once they saw Suho running across the steppes toward them, carrying
something white in his arms.

When they dashed out to meet him, they saw that the white object was a newborn foal.

Beaming with happiness, Suho told them of his adventure.

"I was just on my way home when I noticed this little one, too weak to stand. I searched all around, but found no one who might be his master, and his mother was nowhere in sight. I was afraid the wolves would find him during the night. So I brought him home."

Days went by, and Suho devoted himself to caring for the colt. It grew into a splendid, spirited yearling. Its coat gleamed as white as a field of snow, and everyone who looked at it admired its beauty. To Suho, the horse was as dear as his own life.

One night Suho was jolted out of sleep by the wild neighing of his horse and the bleating of his sheep. He sprang out of bed and ran to the sheepfold where he penned his flock at night. He saw a huge wolf trying to leap the fence and attack the sheep. But the white horse faced the wolf and with desperate bravery did its best to fight off the attacker.

After Suho had driven the wolf away, he hurried back to the sheepfold.
The young horse was shivering and dripping with sweat.
Suho gave his horse a good rubdown and spoke to it as if to a brother.
"White horse! You fought well and bravely tonight. I thank you!"

Months flew past, and soon they became years.

One spring exciting news spread among all the shepherds.

The governor had declared that a big race was to be held in the city. As a prize, the winner might claim the hand of the governor's daughter as his bride.

The shepherds of Suho's village urged him, "You have such a fine white horse! Why not enter the race?"

So Suho mounted his beloved white horse and rode off across the wide grasslands.

A crowd of spectators had already gathered at the field. In a large pavilion beside the racetrack sat the richly dressed, fat governor, surrounded by his guards and other noblemen.

From all over the country bold young horsemen had come to enter the race. The signal was given. With one accord, they swung their leather riding crops and galloped off. The race had begun.

Onward the horses ran, as swift as birds in flight. One horse
led the field. It was Suho's white horse.

"The white horse has won. Go and summon its rider," commanded the governor.

But when Suho was brought forward, the governor saw he was only a poor shepherd boy. Ignoring his promise to make the winner his son-in-law, he grunted, "I shall give you three pieces of silver. You are to leave the white horse with me. Now get out of my sight."

Angrily Suho retorted, "I came here to run in a race! I did not come to barter horseflesh."

"Insolent beggar! You dare answer me back?" the governor shouted.
"Guards! Throw him out!

The guards rushed out to obey their master's command. Suho was beaten
and left lying senseless where he had fallen.

Leading the white horse, the governor called his men to him
and haughtily left the field.

Suho was rescued and carried home by one of his comrades.

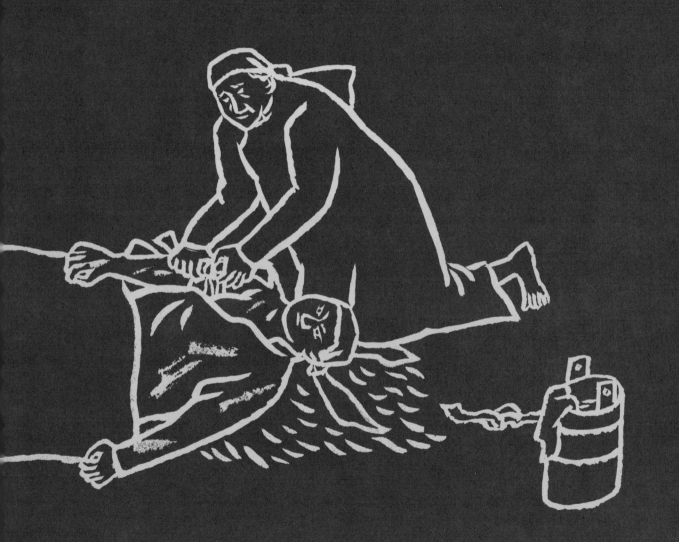

Suho was badly hurt. Lovingly and skillfully his grandmother tended him. Her care eventually brought healing to Suho's wounds. But nothing could heal the sorrow in his heart.

What had become of his white horse? Suho could think of nothing else.

Meanwhile the governor felt very pleased with himself for having secured such a swift and handsome horse. He could hardly wait to show it off. One day he invited all the nobles to a grand banquet.

When the feast was at its height, his men led out the white horse, richly saddled and bridled. The governor intended to ride the horse then and there, for all his guests to admire.

He heaved himself into the saddle.

Suddenly the horse began to buck and rear, and the fat governor thudded to the ground. The horse flashed through the noisy throng and galloped off, swift as the wind on the steppes.

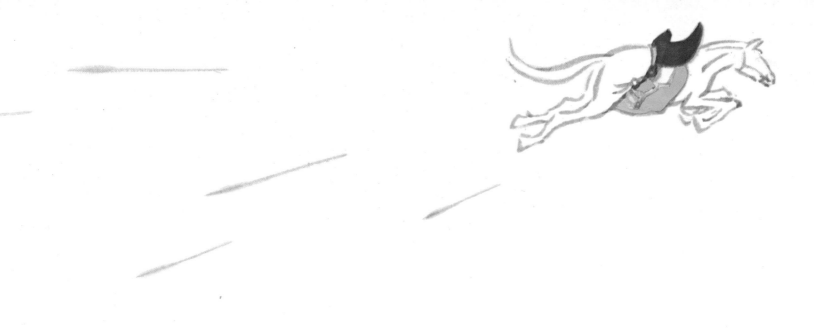

The governor struggled to his feet. "Quick!" he bellowed. "Go after that horse! If you can't catch him, then take your bows and shoot him! Don't let him get away alive!"

The guards drew their bows. One after another, the arrows struck home in the horse's flanks. But he still raced on.

Late that evening Suho heard a noise outside the tent.

"Who is there?" he called. No answer came—only the same noise again.

Suho's grandmother went outside.

"The horse!" she cried. "It is our white horse!"

Suho jumped up and rushed out. It was indeed his white horse,
with arrows bristling from its back and sweat pouring from its body.
    In spite of the cruel arrow wounds, the horse had galloped on and on,
until it was safe again with the kind master whom it loved so much.

Gritting his teeth, Suho pulled the arrows one by one out of the horse's flanks.

"White horse! My own white horse! Do not leave me alone again—do not die!"

But the horse grew weaker, and in its large eyes the luster faded.

The horse died early the next day.

Shattered by sorrow, Suho lay sleepless night after night. Finally there came a night when he dozed off into a fitful sleep. The white horse appeared to him in a dream. When Suho stroked it, it drew close to him and nuzzled him fondly.

"Suho," it said in a soft voice, "you must not mourn for me so. Take my bones, hide, and sinews, and use them to make an instrument to play upon. If you do this, then I will be able to stay by your side forever and will always bring you peace and delight."

The moment Suho awoke, he set about making a new kind of musical instrument. He did just as the white horse had told him to do, fashioning the instrument from the bones, sinews, hide, and hair of his beloved horse.

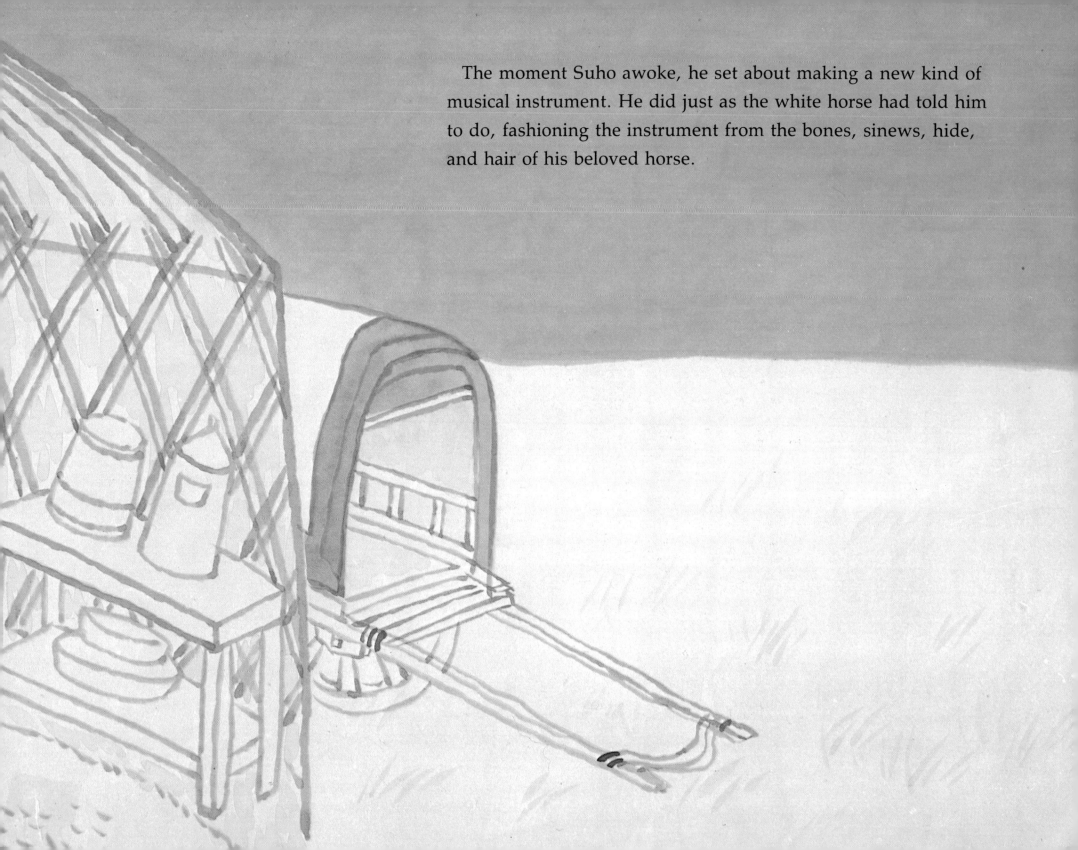

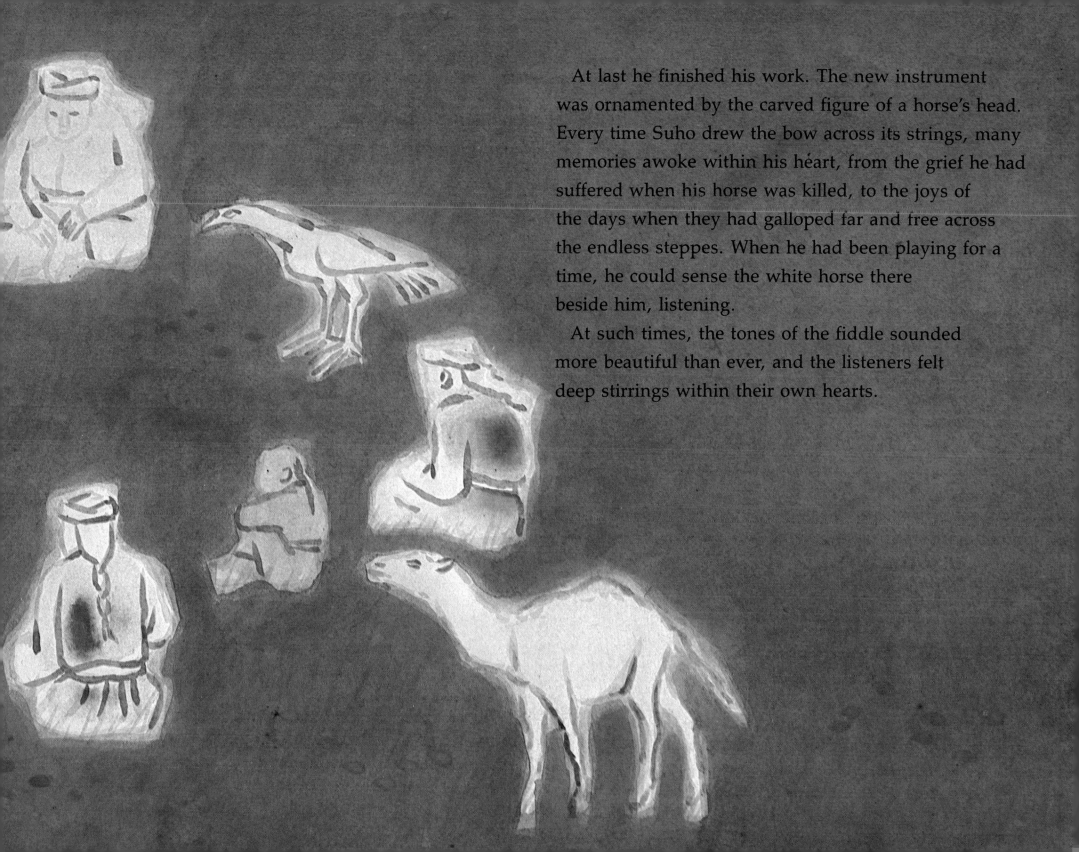

At last he finished his work. The new instrument was ornamented by the carved figure of a horse's head. Every time Suho drew the bow across its strings, many memories awoke within his heart, from the grief he had suffered when his horse was killed, to the joys of the days when they had galloped far and free across the endless steppes. When he had been playing for a time, he could sense the white horse there beside him, listening.

At such times, the tones of the fiddle sounded more beautiful than ever, and the listeners felt deep stirrings within their own hearts.

Others made horse-head fiddles like the one Suho
had created. In time its music could be heard in
almost every part of the grasslands of Mongolia.
In the evening, when the day's work had ended, the
shepherds would gather and listen to the song the
horse-head fiddle sang. They forgot their weariness,
and their hearts grew warm with peace and delight,
giving them new strength for the days to come.

English translation Copyright © 1981 by Fukuinkan Shoten / Illustrations Copyright © 1967
by Fukuinkan Shoten / All rights reserved / First published in 1981 by The Viking Press,
40 West 23rd Street, New York, New York 10010 / Published simultaneously in Canada by
Penguin Books Canada Limited / Printed in Japan

2   3   4   5   6   88   87   86   85   84

Library of Congress Cataloging in Publication Data
Ōtsuka, Yūzō, 1921–   Suho and the white horse.
Translation of Sūho no shiroi uma.
Summary: Relates how the tragic parting of a boy and his horse led to the creation of
the horsehead fiddle of the Mongolian shepherds.
[1. Folklore—Mongolia]   I. Akaba, Suekichi.   II. Title.
PZ8.1.O84Su   1981   398.2'0951'7   [E]   80-26789   ISBN 0-670-68149-0